Richard Sc

FLOATING
BANANAS

A GOLDEN BOOK • NEW YORK
Western Publishing Company, Inc., Racine, Wisconsin 53404

© 1993 Richard Scarry. Published with the authorization of Les Livres du Dragon d'Or.
All rights reserved. Printed in the U.S.A. No part of this book may be reproduced or copied
in any form without written permission from the publisher. All trademarks are the property
of Western Publishing Company, Inc. Library of Congress Catalog Card Number: 93-78418
ISBN: 0-307-30139-7 MCMXCIV

OBSOLETE
NOT FOR SALE

Bananas Gorilla is driving his bananamobile.

He sees a bunch of bananas hanging outside the grocery store.

"I'd like to grab those bananas," he says. "I just LOVE to eat bananas!"

But Sergeant Murphy is nearby.

"Good morning!" Bananas Gorilla says with a smile.
"Good morning!" Sergeant Murphy replies.

Soon Bananas Gorilla meets
Huckle and Lowly Worm.
   They are both eating bananas.
   Bananas Gorilla stops his
bananamobile.

"Hey, where did you get
those bananas?" he asks.

"There is a banana boat in the harbor today,"
Huckle replies. "The captain gave us the bananas."

"WOW!" says Bananas Gorilla.
"I have to see that!"
He speeds away.

A big yellow ship is tied to the Busytown dock. On the side is written BANANAS.

That evening Captain Anteater leaves the ship to have dinner at Louie's restaurant.

He orders a dandelion salad.

"It will be delicious, I'm sure!" Captain Anteater tells Louie. "And a nice change from the food aboard ship!"

"What do you eat on the ship?" asks Louie.

"Fried bananas, boiled bananas, banana salad, and banana splits," replies Captain Anteater.

After dinner Captain Anteater returns happily
to his ship and goes to sleep.

When Captain Anteater
wakes up the next morning,
he sees banana peels floating
all over the harbor.

"Someone has been eating my bananas!"
he shouts. He calls Sergeant Murphy.
When Sergeant Murphy arrives, he
sees the bananamobile parked on the dock.

"I think I know who our thief is," Sergeant Murphy tells the captain, "and where to find him!"

Sergeant Murphy begins to search the ship for the thief.

He looks on deck.
He looks in the lifeboats.

He looks down the smokestack, but he doesn't find Bananas Gorilla.

Sergeant Murphy asks Waveband the radioman
if he has seen a gorilla on board.
"Why, yes, I have," replies Waveband. "Follow me."

They walk down a corridor to a door marked CREW.
"Here you are, sir," Waveband says, saluting.

Sergeant Murphy opens the door.
The crew is inside, dozing on bunks and playing cards. They are all gorillas!

"Um, excuse me," says Sergeant Murphy, shutting the door again quietly.

Then Sergeant Murphy searches the engine room and the hold. Finally he comes to a door marked KITCHEN.

He opens the door.
There is Bananas Gorilla,
tossing a banana peel out of
a porthole.

"Stop, thief!" shouts
Sergeant Murphy as
he rushes in.

"Just a minute!" says Cookie the chef. "That's no thief. That's my assistant. We are trying a new recipe."

Cookie sniffs a big,
bubbling pot.
   Bananas Gorilla tosses
in another banana.
"Banana soup!"

At dinner that evening the crew agrees that
Bananas Gorilla makes the best banana soup ever!